Don't Slam the Door!

Holly Green

ILLUSTRATED BY
Sarah Chamberlin Scott

PUBLISHING WORKS
EXETER, NEW HAMPSHIRE
2005

Illustrations copyright © 2005 by Sarah Chamberlin Scott.

Book and cover design: Sally Reed, The Quick Brown Fox, Groton, MA

A portion of the proceeds from the sale of this book will be donated to the ongoing research to find a cure for Huntington's Disease.

Published by

PublishingWorks
4 Franklin Street
Exeter, NH 03833
800/333-9883
www.publishingworks.com

Library of Congress Cataloging-in-Publication Data

Green, Holly, 1957-
    Don't slam the door! / Holly Green ; illustrated by Sarah Chamberlin Scott.
    p. cm.
    Summary: All summer long at their grandfather's cabin, five sisters must listen to Grandpa's cranky reminders about slamming the door, until eventually the girls come up with an inventive solution to the problem. Includes information about Huntington's disease.
    ISBN: 0-9744803-7-1
    [1. Grandfathers–Fiction. 2. Sisters–Fiction. 3. Vacation homes–Fiction.
4. Summer–Fiction. 5. Huntington's chorea.] I. Title: Do not slam the door!.
II. Scott, Sarah Chamberlin, ill. III. Title.

PZ7.G82273Do2004   2004060058
[E]—dc21

Printed in Canada

DEDICATED TO MY BRILLIANT,
TALENTED AND BEAUTIFUL DAUGHTER,
HEATHER JAYNE RENNIE

Acknowledgments

I have been blessed to be working with a very talented professional: Jeremy Townsend, my publisher.

Perhaps the most deserving of praise is the illustrator, Sarah Chamberlin Scott, who, having been afflicted by polio at a young age, is able to work only with her left hand. Her artwork is among the most beautiful I have ever encountered. We are both handicapped in different ways; however, together we have completed this book. I believe that when God closes a door, He opens another. Amen!

This book would not have been written without the input and collection of memories from all of my sisters: Kerry Green, Stacey Dils, Betsy Green and Sally Cameron.

Marlea Hawkins-Trevino, a Ph.D. candidate, a great friend, and past president of our book club, who has acted as my editor throughout this entire process. Her entire family has given me input on this book: Milton, Ursula, Yliana, Sophia, and Ramiro.

My other dear friends who supported me through this venture are Maureen Scheelar and her entire family: Mary-Lincoln Neely, Karen Florio, Eileen McNeely, and Mary Santry Brodsky.

Also to Heather's dad, Paul Rennie, for his expert technical assistance, and to all the children, either nieces or nephews or godchildren, who sat and listened to this story again and again before it became a book: John Max Holland, Karalyn and Hugh Rennie, Drew and Colin Mitchell, Charlotte and John Put, and Christopher Brodskey, Trey, Hope and McCall Scheeler. Many thanks to all!

— Holly Green

WHEN I WAS A LITTLE GIRL, every summer my four sisters and my mom and dad and I would pile into the family station wagon to make our yearly trip to Grandpa's Cabin on East Kenoza Place. All seven of us with our two cocker spaniels enjoyed a long, noisy ride on a big highway.

The town where Grandpa lived
during the summer was called
Smallwood because it was very
small—almost no one lived there.
The town was surrounded by majestic
mountains and was filled with tall,
beautiful pine trees.

Before we arrived at Grandpa's
cabin, my father would always remind
us, "Please remember not to slam the
door." Grandpa's backdoor made a
loud noise if it wasn't closed properly.
If any of us forgot, Grandpa would
turn cranky and say, "Don't slam the
door!"

Grandpa was a widower. He had lost his lovely wife to a mean and nasty sickness called Huntington's disease. Grandma had convinced him to build this cabin many years ago, before she was ill. They spent their summers there. The cabin had no phone, no TV, no shower, no bathtub and no heat! But it was filled with memories. On cold mornings, Grandpa would build a fire in the big stone fireplace.

Grandpa's cabin
was built backward
with the front porch
in the back and the
backyard in the front.
On the porch were
musty, old rocking
chairs, perfect for
reading in and
watching the rain.
The cabin was
painted spruce green,
and in the yard there
was a huge oak tree.
Grandpa had built
two swings that hung
from the branches.
Up and down, back
and forth, we would
swing all day.

All day long my sisters and I would go in and out of the cabin for lemonade and in and out for cookies, and every time Grandpa would say, "Don't slam the door!"

Sometimes our cousin John, who was nicknamed Outrageous, would visit. We'd all go fishing in Catfish Pond. First we had to dig for worms in the mucky yard and collect them in tin coffee cans for our bait. Then, as we left for our expedition, Grandpa would say, "Don't slam the door!"

If there were a boat docked at the lake, John would say, "Hop in!"

I, being the oldest, would hesitate. "But this is not our boat!" I worried.

"We're just going to borrow it," he'd reply, and off we'd go for an adventure.

One time, all six of us jumped into
a big rowboat with our fishing gear.
We were rowing out of the cove
when a man startled us. "Stop! You're
using my boat!" he yelled. We had to
return the boat, apologize, and retreat
to the cabin, only to hear "Don't slam
the door!"

When we arrived at the cabin for
dinner each evening, the mosquitos
were biting and we would all rush
onto the porch.

Grandpa would say, "Don't slam the
door!"

Dinner was always either meatloaf or spaghetti.

After dinner were unending games
of checkers and cards.

All season long, aunts, uncles and grandkids would visit. Sometimes as many as ten people would sleep over at the same time. There were never enough beds available for everyone. Any child five years old or younger would have to sleep in a crib. And if any of us misbehaved, we were warned we'd have to stay all summer, hearing "Don't slam the door!"

One year, the door-slamming seemed to be a particular problem for Grandpa and his guest relatives. We grandkids realized that something must be done if we were to get through the summer in peace.

All five of us walked to the local town center, which had only a post office, a gas station and a candy store. There we each bought a pack of Bazooka Bubblegum and went home to hear, "Don't slam the door!"

We all began to chew, chew, chew, chew, and chew. Each of us made our own big fat wad of gum, and we stuck them all together.

As the adults took their afternoon naps, I stuck our sticky blob as high up on the backdoor as I could reach. Amazingly, our plan worked. The gum kept the door from banging.

And we never heard, "Don't slam the door!" again.

As I visit my grandfather's now antique cabin, I remember all the family members who spent so much time playing here who are no longer with us. I also remember how much I love them and miss them. That is what memories are all about.

Thank you for letting me share mine with you.

EPILOGUE

My grandmother was disabled by Huntington's Disease. She could not get around at all except in a wheelchair, and she could not speak. She would pat us on the head as a way of communicating with us. Even though she could not speak, she could hear and fully understand what was happening. She died when I was seven years old. My grandfather cared for her, their four children, and later on, their fifteen grandchildren until his death at age ninety-two. His cabin, which is located in the Catskill Mountains of New York, still stands.

At age forty-five, I too was diagnosed with Huntington's Disease, the disease which afflicted my grandmother and my father. Now my goal is to help some very dedicated researchers find a cure for this disease as soon as possible. I volunteer my free time to help in the research programs on Huntington's, and hope to educate people about this illness. A portion of the proceeds from this book are going to the ongoing research to find a cure for Huntington's disease.

Currently, I am the only person in my entire family who has tested positive for this disease and I am praying that I am the last one to suffer from it.

Marjorie Guthrie, mother of Arlo and wife of Woody, used three interconnecting circles to describe Huntington's disease. Some patients have problems in all three of these areas; some have severe problems and some do not. Some may not have any problems for a long time.

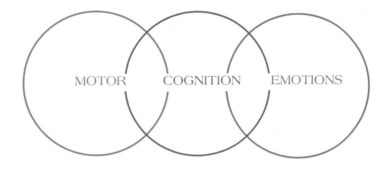

MOTOR   COGNITION   EMOTIONS

At this time, there is no cure for this neuro-logical disease; however, there are incredibly talented medical professionals working day and night to find a cure as well as caring for their patients.

For more information on Huntington's please visit this web site: www.hdny.org.